For my friend, Phoebe Gilman.
F.W.

For Gabriel and Apple, with thanks to Dr Hok.
N.L.

Scholastic Canada Ltd.
175 Hillmount Road, Markham, Ontario L6C 1Z7, Canada

Scholastic Inc.
555 Broadway, New York, NY 10012, USA

Scholastic Australia Pty Limited
PO Box 579, Gosford, NSW 2250, Australia

Scholastic New Zealand Limited
Private Bag 94407, Greenmount, Auckland, New Zealand

Scholastic Ltd.
Villiers House, Clarendon Avenue, Leamington Spa,
Warwickshire CV32 5PR, UK

The illustrations for this book were created using pen, ink, pencil, paint, and an Apple
Macintosh computer.

Library of Canada Cataloguing in Publication

Wishinsky, Frieda
        Jennifer Jones won't leave me alone / Frieda Wishinsky ; illustrations by
Neal Layton.

Originally published: Toronto : HarperCollins, 1995.
ISBN 0-439-96981-6

        I. Layton, Neal II. Title.

PS8595.I834J45 2004   jC813'.54   C2003-905217-6

No part of this publication may be reproduced or stored in a retrieval system, or
transmitted in any form or by any means, electronic, mechanical, recording, or
otherwise, without written permission of the publisher, Scholastic Canada Ltd.,
175 Hillmount Road, Markham, Ontario L6C 1Z7, Canada. In the case of photocopying
or other reprographic copying, a licence must be obtained from Access Copyright
(Canadian Copyright Licensing Agency), 1 Yonge Street, Suite 1900, Toronto, Ontario
M5E 1E5 (1-800-893-5777).

6 5 4 3 2   Printed in Singapore   05 06 07

Jennifer Jones

Jones

won't Leave Me Alone

Frieda wishinsky

Neal Layton

Scholastic Canada Ltd.

Jennifer Jones won't leave me alone.
She sits by my side.
She **SHOUTS** in my ear.

She tells me she loves me.
She calls me her "dear."

She writes me love poems
Full of words like **adore**
Then she sticks on red hearts
She bought at the store.

And my friends laugh and snicker.
They point and they stare.
They say,

WELL, WE DON'T AND I HATE IT!

I've had quite enough.
I wish that she'd move
And take all her stuff.

She could move to the jungle
And live in a tree

And talk to the monkeys,
Instead of to me.

But if she insists
That she's not going there,

She could head for the Arctic
And bother a bear.

Or fly to
the desert

Or go to the moon.

I really don't care,
As long as it's soon.

Hurrah! Hallelujah!

Guess what I just heard?
Jennifer's moving.
Her mum's been transferred.

"I'll miss you,"
She said with a
tear in her eye.
Then she gave me
a kiss
And whispered,

"Goodbye."

Now her seat is all empty.
There's nobody there.
There's no one to kiss me.

There's no one to care.

So I write in my notebook.
I add and subtract.
I study my spelling.
I learn a new fact.

But it's boring! It's lonely!
I miss her a lot.
I wish she'd return

To her usual spot .

And to make matters worse
She writes:

It's divine
Seeing paris at night,

sailing boats down the Rhine,

Nibbling Viennese pastries you can't get at home.

Oh, she's having such fun,
I thought in despair.

She'll never come home.
She'll stay over there.

But then I read on,
"I'll see you in June."
And I yelled,

"WHOOP-
DEE
DOO!!!

She'll return very soon."

But I told them the truth
As I opened the door,
And I ran off to buy

Red hearts
at the store.